Introduction

Dilo was a dolphin, who was always poking his nose, or more correctly his beak, into everything. He was intensely curious and liked to know what was going on. From the moment he came into the undersea world Dilo brought joy into his mother's life. But Dilo was not just her baby, he was also her friend. Dilo had a star on his dorsal fin. Only those who could see it knew he had a special mission.

HORACE DOBBS

and the
Call of the Deep

Illustrated by Rico

First Published in 1994

Reprinted 1998
(with revisions)
by
Watch Publishing
'Dolphin'
10 Melton Road
North Ferriby
E Yorks HU14 3ET
England
Tel: 01482 643403
Fax: 01482 634914

A catalogue record for this book is available
from the British Library

ISBN
0 9522389 5 0
Copyright Horace Dobbs
© 1998

Printed by
Redcliff Studios
30 The Weir
Hessle
East Yorkshire
HU13 ORU
Tel: 01482 640428 Fax: 01482 641390

Contents

Introduction
Dedication

Dedications

This book is for *Fiona and Rebecca Parker* - the most wonderful grandchildren I could ever wish to have - who constantly remind me how sad it is that we all have to grow up.

This book is also for *Kerry Oldfield* to celebrate the visit she made to Dingle with her father Richard Oldfield, alias Rico, who illustrated this book. In Ireland they had some memorable encounters with a friendly wild dolphin named Funghie.

1 The mysterious monster

Only a short time before Dilo was born, his mother had been with two other dolphins who had been her companions for a long time. They stayed as a group and spent much of their time playing together. They would rush through the water before jumping high into the sky. Sometimes they would get very excited and deliberately bump into one another.

One day Dilo's mother received an extra hard bump which hurt her. She swam away from her friends - but they chased after her, thinking she was enjoying the extra rough game. When she squeaked in protest they rushed at her all the more until she became angry, which is very unusual for a dolphin. Her companions were surprised by her change of mood. They hung together sorrowfully in the water.

It was almost time to start feeding. So Dilo's mother, feeling upset, swam away to go fishing on her own. She left the area of sea in which there were many fish to be found and had to swim a long way to find another place where food was plentiful. She needed to eat more than usual because of the baby dolphin growing inside her.

When she had eaten her fill, she started to make her way back to the place where the three dolphins usually gathered to play. She was feeling happy and looking forward to a good romp with her friends. She speeded up as she approached, and sent out a call into the water to tell them that she was back.

Her call was not answered.

At first she was unconcerned. They were playing a trick on her, weren't they? Hiding away somewhere and keeping silent. She imagined them laughing to themselves as they swam silently through the water not heeding her call. Indeed, the more she thought about it, the more certain she became that they were playing a joke on her. So she hurled herself towards the surface of the sea and jumped high into the sky, as she would have done if all three of them had been together.

When darkness began to fall, her sense of fun deserted her. A joke was a joke, but this was no longer funny. Dilo's mother started to feel lonely. She called again and again into the water, pleading for her friends to return - but all she heard were the night sounds of the ocean and the distant rumblings of a machine.

By the time the sun rose again into the heavens she knew something was wrong. Surely they wouldn't go far and leave her. Why were they so silent? Why were they not in the place where they usually played together? What had happened?

Like all dolphins, Dilo's mother could locate things too far away to see underwater by sending out a special sound and listening for the echo. She set off towards their customary fishing grounds, calling, and calling again. Something strange had happened. The echo that came back told Dilo's mother that there were no big shoals of fish and no sign of her two companions. She noticed that some of the fishes in the area were injured and swam about in circles. She could easily have caught them, but she did not feel hungry. She searched the seabed for clues, and found some dead fishes; never before had she seen so many with crabs crawling over them and biting into them with their claws.

Feeling desperate she sent more and more signals across the seabed. At last one of the echoes that came faintly back told her what she had been looking for. She rushed forward though the green water, the special echo becoming stronger and stronger. Then suddenly she spotted one of her companions. She stopped using her echo sound and just looked at him closely with her eyes.

He was lying between two rocks and did not move. She swam slowly past and listened for sounds of life inside him, but there were none. She pushed her beak under the dolphin and tried to lift his body towards the surface so that he could get some air, but he rolled over and fell back to the sand, where he lay still on his side. Dilo's mother saw marks on him, as if he had been in a great fight. The marks were certainly not from playing with other dolphins. They looked as if they had been made by a strange monster. Could it be the monster they had been warned about but never seen? Had the monster also killed the fish she had seen on the seabed?

Dilo's mother felt very sad and miserable and tried again to push her companion up to the surface for air, but he flopped back to the seabed. She sent out a call for help but no friendly response came back.

Desperately lonely, she circled round and round her dead friend. Darkness came again, and still she stayed. She would rise to take a breath only when she had to, and then would sink slowly back filled with grief. What kind of monster could have done this to her beautiful friend?

On the seabed she spotted some of the night- creatures beginning to prowl. She heard the slithering sound she knew was made by an eel. From out of a hole in the rocks popped a head, and then slowly, like a snake, emerged a long black body. Suddenly, as if fired by a spring, the eel rushed forward and bit hard into the dead dolphin with its sharp teeth, then spinning like a top it tried to tear a piece of flesh from the body. Dilo's mother was filled with rage. She hurled herself at the eel and hit it with her beak, sending it reeling through the water. The startled eel writhed and twisted into a coil. There was no need for a second attack. As the eel rapidly uncoiled itself and slithered back into its hole in the rocks, her anger subsided as quickly as it had come. She knew the eel had not killed the dolphin. It was only doing what eels always do - dispose of the bodies of other creatures.

The lively spirit of her dolphin companion had gone . All that was left of his body would have to go back into the cycle of the sea. Dilo's mother knew about these things. She did not know however about the mysterious monster that had split the body from its spirit. Would the monster come back and attack her? It was time to move elsewhere.

Slowly, sadly, she swam away. She moved as quietly as she could, barely breaking the surface to take a breath and staying underwater for long periods. She moved so quietly that any humans nearby would not have seen her pass.

2 A drink of milk

Dilo's mother remained stricken with grief until one day she felt a stirring deep inside her. When it passed she thought she must have eaten something bad. Then it happened again, and again. At first she tried to ignore it, but when each urge came quicker and quicker she knew her baby was about to be born. She swam into a place where the water was calm and shallow, and then rose to the surface, taking a deep breath before slowly sinking down again, letting her body relax completely. When the next urge came she pushed with the muscles inside her. As she did so a tiny tail came out of her body. She relaxed and then pushed again. Dilo slipped gently into the sea - a new dolphin was born.

Dilo's mother felt relief and closed her eyes briefly. When she opened them, and saw her baby

for the first time, her entire body seemed as if it was filled with pride and love. The baby dolphin was joined to his mother by a cord. She stayed still and watched. The baby wriggled. Then quite instinctively Dilo's mother rolled quickly and the cord broke. She pushed Dilo to the surface. The newborn dolphin took a breath, opened his eyes and saw a grey shape alongside him. He swam towards his mother and felt her smooth skin with his flipper. Then the two of them sank just below the surface of the sea, and for the first time Dilo was aware of the gentle touch of water as it flowed past and caressed him. He flicked his tail and moved forward. He was soon pushed up to the surface again. As the top of his head burst through into the air, he took another quick gulp of air through the blowhole on the top of his head. Then he flexed his tail hard and rushed forward into the blue-green water with his mother close by his side.

There was something quite unique about Dilo. His mother didn't notice it at first. Gradually it became clearer. Dilo had a star on his dorsal fin.

From the moment he was born Dilo seemed to glow with joy, When Dilo touched his mother she felt great pleasure. With her new baby by her side, all the sadness she experienced before he was born vanished like a bubble bursting.

Dilo did not have to be pushed up to the surface again. Something inside always told him when to rise to take a breath of air.

17

Dilo loved to stroke his mother with his flippers and nuzzle her with the tip of his beak. Her skin was neither hard nor cold. It was very smooth but wasn't slippery. When he touched his mother, Dilo felt good inside.

Dilo stayed close by his mother. As they swam slowly along together, she knew that, although he could swim and dive and take air without lessons, there were many things she would have to teach him. She would have to tell him about the moon and how it made the tides flow. She would have to teach him how to ride in waves, how he could find his way across the big deserts of the sandy seabeds and through the undersea mountains where rocks rise up from the sand. She would show him great forests of seaweed. All that would come later. First he must learn to feed.

When he was fully-grown, Dilo would catch fish, but until then he would feed on his mother's milk. So she encouraged Dilo to press against her. In a very short time Dilo discovered that if he

pushed his beak against a certain place on the underside of his mother it would open and creamy rich milk would flow into him, especially when he curled his soft pink tongue into a tube. When he moved away the opening shut and the little teat from which the milk flowed disappeared.

After that, although he rubbed his little beak all over his mother's body, he found only two places near her tail where there was milk, and he often returned to them to enjoy the pleasure of food. Sometimes he would stay so long that he would run out of breath, and then he would have to rush to the surface to gulp some air.

He once tried to suck in air through his mouth, like he did milk, but it left him gasping. He was learning that dolphins can only breathe through their blowholes which open when they breathe out and shut tightly after they have breathed in. Being a very curious dolphin, Dilo wondered what would happen if he kept his blowhole open after breathing in. When he tried it, water rushed in and made him choke. He blew

out hard, sending a cloud of spray into the air. He closed his blowhole immediately he had taken his next breath, and stayed just below the surface until he was sure it would not let in any more water. That was enough experimenting for one day.

Dilo dived down and nuzzled into his mother. She had been watching him and was very amused, but she pretended she had not seen what he was doing. Dilo liked being close to his mother and feeding from her. It made him feel safe and secure. He was aware there were dangers all around, but when he was very close to her he felt that nothing in the world could harm him.

3 Dilo's magic power

There were times when the sea became cloudy and Dilo could not see very far underwater. He soon discovered that this did not matter because he had a very special magic power. It told him what was in front of him, even when he could not detect it with his eyes. Dilo would make a sound that only dolphins can make and send it out into the sea; then he would listen. When the sound came back it was like an echo but different, and told him what was there. The sound echoed so quickly it was almost like switching on a powerful torch in the darkness. So special was his magic power that it also told him what things were made of and what was inside them.

From the moment Dilo was born his mother talked to him. She did not use words, or sentences, or anything like human speech, so it would be correct to say she communicated with him. Sometimes she would use sound pictures. When she saw a fish, Dilo's mother would send out a sound beam and the echo would give her a sound picture. If she wanted to tell Dilo about the fish she would mimic the echo and he would see the fish as if with his own magic sound beam. Slowly Dilo learnt how to make sound pictures himself. That was just one of the things he was learning as he grew up. There were many more.

The seabed in the bay where Dilo was born was mostly flat and sandy. There were also many rocks covered with seaweed. At the edge of the bay a huge rock rose right out of the sea and disappeared into the other world above them. That was the strange world where they went to get a breath of air. When he rose to the surface near the rock Dilo could see strange animals moving through the air.

"That rock is called Gull Rock," Dilo's mother informed him.

"It is part of what we call 'The Other World'.

One day I will tell you about 'The Other World'. But first you must learn about our own world in the sea. Come with me and I will show you."

Dilo and his mother set off together to swim over the sandy seabed around the bay. Before long they came across a small comical creature walking sideways on six armoured legs. When the creature saw them coming, it moved faster and faster until it was running so fast that its feet seemed barely to touch the sand. But it could not run as fast as dolphins can swim, and in a moment they were over the top of it, looking down on front nippers waving up towards them.

Dilo's mother told him it was a swimming crab.

"Good morning Swimming Crab, " said Dilo in his own language which nobody, not even his mother, understood.

Dilo felt pleased with himself. He pretended he knew all about crabs. He heard a soft "Grrrr, Grrr, Grrr" sound coming through the water, and without waiting to ask his mother, Dilo dived down to touch the crab with his beak. The crab grabbed hold of Dilo's beak as tight as it could with one of its sharp nippers, and hung on.

"Ouch!" shrieked Dilo as he swam back to his mother with the crab still pinching his beak and clinging on ot it.

Dilo's mother looked at him - her eyes shining bright with laughter because he looked so funny.

"Ouch," shouted Dilo again, shaking his head. When he did this the crab let go and swam to the seabed, where its back legs began to work faster than ever. Dilo watched in amazement, for in what seemed like no time at all the little creature vanished from view.

Dilo stayed very close to his mother touching her with his flippers. He could feel her laughter.

"You must learn," she said, "that when a crab waves at you with its claws it is not a sign of welcome."

"What does it mean then?" enquired Dilo.

"Keep away, or I will pinch you."

"Oh, " said Dilo.

Then after a few moments he enquired,

"Where has it gone?"

"It's gone down into the 'Undersand World'. There are many creatures down there. Lots of them have shells. Come on, let's see if we can find one that won't bite you."

Dilo stayed close beside his mother as she

moved slowly over the sand. He could hear her making a creaking sound as she went. Then suddenly he heard the note of the creak change.

"Stop here" she signalled. "Can you see that row of tiny bright eyes over there?" Dilo peered at the sand.

"No I can't," he said, still looking as hard as he could.

"Then watch carefully with your eyes as well as using your echo-sound."

Dilo's mother moved forward and dived gently towards the seabed. Just before she reached the bottom Dilo spotted the row of bright sparkling eyes. Then they vanished as the shell snapped shut like the lid of a box. Dilo's mother swam down and nudged the shell with her beak.

With a "clop", "clop", "clop", it lifted off the seabed. Opening and closing rapidly, the shell bobbed through the water for a short distance and then dropped back down again - as if it were exhausted. It was tightly shut and Dilo could see the shell very clearly now.

"I can't see the eyes any more," said Dilo.

"That is because the shell is frightened and is shut. It won't open until we have gone away," she continued.

"Can all shellfish swim like that?" asked Dilo.

"Oh no, that is one of a few that can," she said, enjoying Dilo's obvious interest in the great scallop as this particular shellfish was called.

"I'm going to see if I can find another one," said Dilo.

He moved forward and made a creaking sound like his mother. When he heard the sound change, he looked forward, and there in front of him was a row of bright eyes. He swam gently towards it to get a closer look. But as his shadow passed over the half-buried shell it shut with a quiet "clop".

Then he heard several more "clops". He looked closely and saw that there was not just one shell, but many of them. When he approached slowly they just stayed still on the seabed. It was not until he fanned them with his flippers that they all decided he was dangerous and tried to swim away.

"Clop", "clop", "clop", "clop". For a short time the undersea world was full of dancing scallops all going "clop". Then they all dropped back down. They were exhausted and stayed still despite Dilo's attempts to fan them into action again with his flippers.

Dilo swam back to his mother.

"Those Clop-Clop shells get tired very quickly," he said.

31

"They are not Clop-Clop shells, they are scallop shells," she replied, sending him a sound picture of a scallop.

"I think Clop-Clop is a better name," said Dilo, mainly because he found it easier to go "clop", "clop", than to make a sound picture of a scallop.

4 Catching shadows

On one of their journeys exploring the bay the two dolphins approached Gull Rock. When they drew near they saw a creature moving across the sand. It was entirely covered in a blue shell that was very strong. To human eyes it would have looked like a knight in armour. Most impressive, however, were the two large claws at the front that looked like weapons. Dilo's mother told her curious son it was a common lobster and that lobsters spend much of their time in holes in the rocks.

The lobster took no notice of them and continued on its journey. Its two claws were stretched out in front.

"I wouldn't like it to bite me with those claws," thought Dilo as they passed by. But that was just what happened a few moments later.

Dilo was peering under the kelp plants that covered the rocks when he saw a small cave. He poked his head inside. It was the home of a huge lobster.

Before Dilo could say or do anything the lobster gave him an almighty bite with one of his powerful claws.

"Yeowee," cried Dilo as he swam back to his mother as fast as he could.

"Didn't I tell you that lobsters usually live in holes!" said his mother.

"Yes," said Dilo, "but you didn't tell me they do not like visitors."

"You have a lot to learn and you will learn by being curious," she replied.

"H'mm, learning by being curious can be very painful," thought Dilo ruefully as he nuzzled closely against his mother's soft, smooth skin for comfort.

Sometimes Dilo was so happy and full of energy that all he wanted to do was jump for joy. One evening, when the sea was calm and the setting sun turned the sky red, Dilo looked up and saw the orange disc of the sun on the silver screen above him. But when he used his echo- sound it seemed as if there was nothing there. He felt the energy build up inside him. The young dolphin raced upwards and hit the circle with his beak. He burst through the surface and the orange water cascaded from his body. For one moment he thought he had touched the sun. But in the fleeting time he spent flying through the air Dilo saw the orange disc high in the sky above him.

"How did that happen?" he asked himself as he gathered his energy to jump even higher.

Next time he would touch the sun in the sky. He jumped time after time but no matter how high he leaped he never reached it.

"Why can I touch the sun on the surface of the sea but not in the sky!" he asked his mother.

"Because it is not on the surface of the sea," she replied.

"But I saw it," replied Dilo, "and I jumped through it."

"Then you can't always believe what you see, can you?" she said.

"Did you see the sun with your echo-sound?"

"No, I didn't."

"Well then, look down there," she continued.

"Tell me what you see."

"I can see my shadow," said Dilo.

"What does your echo-sound show you?" Dilo's mother asked.

Dilo turned his magic sound on to the

shadow, but no echo came back.

"Go down, pick up your shadow and bring it up to me," Dilo's mother requested.

Always willing to do what was asked of him, Dilo rushed down to his shadow and tried to grab it in his beak. All he got was a mouthful of sand. He tried swimming away from it, but no matter how fast he rushed forwards or backwards his shadow always stayed with him. He swam back to his mother and touched her lovingly with his fin.

37

When he looked down he saw that their shadows were joined together even though they themselves were not touching one another.

"You're right" he said, "everything is not what it appears to be."

5 The sky at night

A big rock that stuck out of the sandy seabed was one of the places Dilo liked most to explore. It had many moods. There were times when he could fly over it. At others it rose right up to the surface and the seaweeds on top poked out into the air. When that happened he had to swim round it. The water near the rock moved in different directions. Sometimes it was very fast. Sometimes it was slow. And sometimes, only briefly, it was quite still.

If Dilo had been human "Why?" would have been his favourite word. He was curious about everything.

"Why is the water sometimes shallow and sometimes deep?" he asked his mother.

"Because of the tides," she replied.

When she told him that the tides were due

39

to "the pull of the moon" he was not at all sure what she meant - but he pretended he did. Even so, Dilo decided to give the moon, or Mister Moon as he preferred to call it, some special attention. He waited until it got quite dark.

Everything was still. The sea heaved gently. Dilo and his mother were resting quietly just beneath the surface. When he looked up Dilo could see lots of little dots of light dancing across the ceiling of his world. He rose slowly so as not to frighten them. But as he touched the surface they disappeared, just iike the sun had, high into the heavens. They looked far away. Far too far away to touch by jumping. Anyway, he didn't feel like jumping. He was in what his mother called one of his "pensive moods".

It looked as if a black cloth had been spread across the sky to block out the sun. But it wasn't a very good cloth because there were lots of holes in it through which the sun managed to shine. But where was Mister Moon? He couldn't see him anywhere.

"Mister Moon hasn't woken up yet," Dilo's mother told him when he returned to her side.

"Look again later."

Sure enough later that night Mister Moon came up over the horizon. Dilo liked Mister Moon. The moon always seemed gentle. Dilo stayed on the surface and swam across the sea watching Mister Moon all of the time. Wherever Dilo went Mister Moon made a path of yellow light across the water straight to him. The dolphin stopped still and gazed at the moon path, wondering how it was that Mister Moon always knew where he was.

"I think Mister Moon is feeling shy tonight," he said to his mother when he returned to her side.

"Oh, why 's that?" she asked.

"Because he is only showing part of his face," replied her son.

Throughout the calm night the two dolphins cruised side by side, sometimes taking brief naps - you see, dolphins don't sleep for long periods like

humans. Often they touched one another with their fins.

When dawn broke Dilo noticed that Mister Moon had climbed much higher into the sky. As the sky turned blue Mister Moon started to fade. One by one the stars went out until there was only one left. Just like the moon it was very pale.

"Mister Moon is going back to sleep and the sun is waking up," Dilo told his mother.

"There is only one star left in the sky."

"That is not a star," Dilo's mother said as they rose to the surface to watch the sunrise together.

"What is it then?"

"It's a planet called Venus."

"How do you know it's not a star?" Dilo asked.

"Because it doesn't twinkle like a star."

"Oh, there is so much I don't know," sighed the young dolphin.

"Don't worry about that," she said, sensing his frustration.

"You can enjoy something as wondrous and beautiful as the night sky without knowing anything about it. But it is more interesting if you do."

Dilo nuzzled up to his mother. She was so wise and comforting. He was enjoying feeling her touch when suddenly she twitched. From far away came the mysterious sound she had heard on the night her companions died. Dilo's mother's mood changed in an instant. She told the young dolphin to stay close by and be very still. She listened intently.

"Don't leave my side for a moment," she said eventually, moving off in the direction opposite to that from which the sound was coming.

Dilo tucked in beside his mother. The two of them swam as if they were one, moving silently and always rising to take a breath together before diving down again.

The sun was very bright and the moon had disappeared completely before they stopped. Dilo's mother listened. The sound had gone. Then much to Dilo's surprise, she accelerated away, threw herself high into the sky, and crashed back into the sea with an enormous splash.

"Come on Dilo," she shouted back at him as if nothing had happened,

"It's time for a game."

6 Nomads

Dilo's mother would often feed close to the cliffs, chasing the fish towards the rocks so they could not escape. Sometimes she would crash her tail onto the surface of the sea to frighten the fish and make them rush out from their hiding places. Dilo always stayed close to his mother and would have to swim as fast as he could to keep up with her. He enjoyed the hunt. He used his echo-sound to find the fish and watched how his mother would catch them in her teeth. She did not chew them but moved them around in her mouth so that they slipped head first down her throat. Swimming close beside her he sped after the fish that twisted and turned and tried to escape. It was not long before he was catching little fish of his own, but sometimes he lost them before he could turn them round to swallow them. Occasionally Dilo's mother would first stun a fish, by shooting a very powerful sound beam at it, before rushing forward and catching it in her mouth.

One of the things Dilo liked most of all was jumping out of the water into the other world. He would swim with all of his might towards the surface and sometimes his tail would still be flapping when he was in the air. His mother told him that dolphins do not leap like that.

"It is not graceful," she said as she showed him how to jump out smoothly and come back into the water with barely a splash.

"Sometimes I like to make a big splash," said Dilo.

"So do I," said his mother, "and I also like to do a backward fall."

"Come and watch me," she said, enjoying the game as much as Dilo. She showed him how. Immediately after, the two dolphins swam down to the seabed together and then rushed to the surface as fast as they could, swimming partly on their backs. They did not leap so high this way but,

when they fell into the sea on their backs, spray flew high and they started new waves. Dilo became so excited he jumped three times on his back in quick succession.

Dilo's mother told him that he must also learn how to be very, very quiet.

"Any dolphin can make a big splash and let everyone know where he is," she said, "but there are times when it is important that nobody should know where you are."

So Dilo practiced going to the surface and taking a breath quietly in the fraction of a second that the top of his head was in the air. Then, without even a tiny splash, he slid silently back into deep water moving his tail slowly. When he did this he could stay underwater for a long time.

Most of the time in which Dilo was under the sea he used his echo-location to find his way around. By sending out beams of sound that were far too high-pitched to be heard by human ears, he could detect everything around him. This was very important at night or during the day when the water was very murky. Indeed, the sound pictures he saw inside his brain when he was echo-locating were so sharp that to human eyes the water would have appeared to be as clear as the cleanest swimming-pool. Thus, by "seeing with sound" Dilo was always able to find fish and swim safely in the dark. He never bumped into rocks, no matter how fast he swam.

Once Dilo was able to catch fish for himself and could swim silently and jump high out of the water in a graceful arc, his mother decided it was time to take him on his first long journey.

"We are the nomads of the sea," she told him.

"What is a nomad?" asked Dilo.

"A nomad does not stay in one place all of the time," said his mother. "Sometimes a nomad will stay in an area for a while and then move on."

"But I like it here - I'm not sure I want to be a nomad," replied Dilo.

"Come with me," said Dilo's Mother.

She took him past Gull Rock and told him to point his head away from the bay.

"Now call with your magic echo-sound," she said to him.

Dilo made the magic sound he used when exploring the bay close to the rocks - but only a very faint reply came back.

"You are not using the right magic sound," his mother said.

So Dilo tried all of the magic sound he could make, and from some of them came a reply.

It was not clear like the reply from the rocks and the fish that were nearby. It had a mysterious quality that made Dilo want to find out what was there.

"That is the Call of the Deep," Dilo's mother told him. Deep inside him Dilo felt something pulling him towards the mysterious water far out to sea.

Then they heard another sound. It was not an echo or a sound of the sea. It had a deep, regular beat. Dilo's mother felt uneasy. She did not know why. The two dolphins waited, listening. Very slowly the sound became quieter as a fishing boat, with its engine throbbing, moved down the coast. Dilo's curiosity was aroused. He wanted to chase after the sound. His mother urged him to be cautious and to resist the temptation to investigate when he heard it again, as he surely would, once they had left the remote bay that had been his first home.

7 Making stars

A few days later Dilo's mother decided it was time to leave.

When Dilo and his mother swam past Gull Rock for the last time the young dolphin felt very excited. The mysteries of the water beyond pulled him like a magnet. He was sad to say goodbye to all the rocks and plants and animals he knew so well.

"Goodbye," he said as he passed the lobster's cave which he remembered particularly well.

The lobster came to the entrance of the cave and waved its claws.

"Grrrr, grrrr," it replied, watching Dilo's tail vanish in the haze.

"Goodbye Clop-Clops," he said when he flew over the sand.

"Clop," "clop," "clop," went the scallop shells in quick succession as the two dolphins passed overhead.

"I'm going to the Call of the Deep. Goodbye, goodbye everyone," called Dilo for the last time.

The sun was shining, the sea was clear blue and the wind blew warm and strong. Dilo and his mother swam just below the surface often rising together to take a breath of air. The tops of some of the waves were covered in pure white foam called white horses or white caps.

"Come on Dilo - I will show you how to ride the waves," said his mother.

She swam up close to the surface just in front of a big wave. Dilo went with her. He discovered that if he stayed just beneath the white cap of the wave he was carried along. Faster and faster he went, enjoying the free ride.

"Whee!" called Dilo, staying very close to his mother who knew where to get the fastest ride.

The bubbles in the foam around them

sparkled like jewels in the bright sunshine. Dilo could feel them against his skin. He was so happy and excited he could not resist rushing forward and leaping right out of a foaming wave.

On and on the two dolphins journeyed together, sometimes riding the white horses, sometimes swimming into the deep clear blue sea, sometimes swimming fast, sometimes swimming slow, but always staying close together.

"Where is the Call of the Deep?" asked Dilo during one of their slow swims.

"It is everywhere around you. It is in the wind. It is in the waves. It is in the deep blue water."

"Oh," said Dilo, realising for the first time that it wasn't a place.

"It's a feeling inside you," continued his mother.

"Where are we going?" he asked, curious to know where they were heading.

"We are going to a place where many seals

live," she replied, "but we have a long way to go yet."

They continued their journey. When the sun set the sea became filled with soft orange light which slowly turned grey and then went out altogether.

Gradually the sea became darker and darker until it was nearly black. Dilo sent out his echo-sound but no message came back. This told him that Seal Island was still a long way off.

When he surfaced he saw the sky was full of stars that glistened in the black heavens. They seemed even further away than the sun. How vast everything was. The sky went on for ever, and so did the sea all around him. He moved closer to his mother. He would not like to be alone in this vast empty space without her. Where did all those stars come from he wondered.

He thought he knew the answer when he looked sideways at his mother for he saw an amazing sight: she was surrounded by thousands

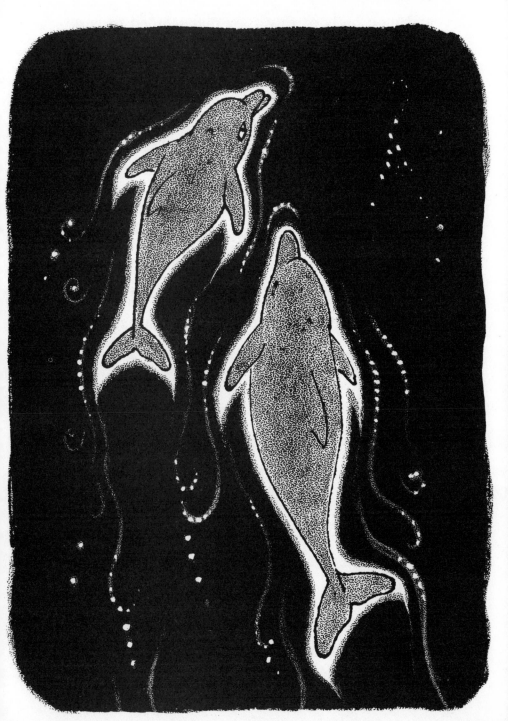

and thousands of tiny stars that seemed to come out of her body and flow past her as she moved through the water. They glowed so brightly he could see her outline shining in the water.

My mother is making stars, he thought to himself.

The stars swirled behind her, marking her passage through the water with a glittering silver trail that faded quickly. How beautiful she looked, surrounded by starlight in the blue-black night.

When she stopped moving, the stars all went out.

"Do all dolphins make stars?" Dilo asked his mother.

"Only on dark nights when they move through the sea" she replied. "They shine especially bright when there is no moon."

Dilo tried to make a sound picture of the sparkling star particles, called phosphorescence, but he couldn't. His mother understood the difficulty he was having expressing himself.

"The sound picture doesn't matter," she said.

"It is what you see and what you think that is important."

"I *saw* you making stars and I *think* it was very beautiful," he replied. "I wish you made stars all of the time."

"Did you know you were also making stars?"

"Was I?" asked Dilo in astonishment.

"Sometimes beautiful things appear very unexpectedly. So you must *always* be ready to see them."

When they moved off again, Dilo caught glimpses of the gleaming speckles in the water all around him which he had not noticed before. The faster he swam the more speckles there were and the more they glowed.

He was so enthralled with the thought of making stars the he forgot all about the empty space beyond.

When the night was over and the sea gradually filled with a pale grey light, the stars around him faded. He rose to the surface and saw that the stars in the sky were also getting dimmer.

"Not everything that is beautiful lasts forever." said Dilo's mother.

Then from far away he heard a sound which he had not heard before. It was a very deep sound, so deep it felt as if the entire sea was vibrating.

8 Giant whales

Dilo's mother had already heard the sound. She moved very close to her son. Dilo could sense that she was excited. She was not at all afraid.

"It is a group of our giant cousins heading back to the feeding grounds," she explained. "They don't chase after fish. They filter their food from the sea with their huge mouths. Come on, let's go and see them."

When she saw a look of decided reluctance on Dilo's face she added, "Don't look so worried, they would never eat *you,* they are far too sensitive to do that. Besides, they don't feed when they're migrating anyway."

Reassured by his mother's obvious knowledge and understanding he tucked in beside her and the two of them sped along to intercept their cousins, the giant whales. Knowing it would be a waste of energy to chase them, she worked out a course that would bring them just in front of the whales. She was saving the events that would follow the encounter as a surprise for Dilo. As they moved ahead Dilo sent out his sound beam. It told him the whales were large. Even so he was amazed at their size when he saw them close to.

His mother had told him they were the biggest creatures ever to live on the planet earth. They gave a roar when they surfaced to breathe, blowing two spouts of spray high into the sky - not one tiny puff like dolphins. Their tail flukes were immensely powerful and moved them through the water deceptively quickly. The group of whales slowed down to make allowance for the

hins and seemed genuinely to like their
company. Despite his inexperience, Dilo was
aware of how gentle and sensitive the giants were.
When Dilo followed his mother past the eye of a
huge whale he felt sure it winked at him. He
could only guess of course because he couldn't see
the other eye.

When the two dolphins were just in front of
a large whale it increased speed. Dilo and his
mother found themselves being carried forward
with no effort at all. Merely by adjusting their
paths with occasional sweeps of their tails, or by
altering the positions of their flippers, the two
dolphins were pushed ahead by the bow wave. It
was a wonderfully exhilarating free ride and it was
the surprise Dilo's mother had been saving for
him. No dolphin could have enjoyed it more.

When the big whale slowed to allow the
other whales to catch up Dilo found himself
surrounded by whales. The vast sea was filled with
their sounds; sounds so powerful they made his body
vibrate. It was as if he was joined to the whales by their

songs and their songs were part of the deep. Dilo felt safe. He wasn't a little dolphin any more. He was as big as the ocean. Life was wonderful.

Then, like a single choirboy in an enormous cathedral pulsing with the music from a giant organ, Dilo's mother heard her son singing - spinning his own thin threads of golden sound into the cloak of joy and security the whales had wrapped around her.

The whales were on a journey to ice-cold polar waters to feed. Seal Island was in a different direction. The whales and dolphins parted company after spending a joyful day together.

The young traveller snuggled up to his mother not knowing he was in for yet another surprise. It started with a deep rumbling sound.

At first Dilo's mother did not want to go to investigate. However, still feeling excited from riding the bow wave of the giant whale, Dilo was keen for more adventures. He persuaded his mother that they should head in the direction of the sound.

When they got close Dilo scanned the source of the noise with his magic sound. Then he surfaced to have a look with his eyes. What he saw was a huge tanker laden with oil. It was much bigger than the biggest of the whales. Unlike the whales, which were flexible and seemed to flow through the water, the giant ship forced its way through with a power so great neither Dilo nor his mother could imagine it.

They approached the vessel from the side, feeling the way the water flowed with their sensitive skins. The two dolphins stayed close together, dived right underneath it and headed towards the bow. Under the front of the vessel was a huge bulb, bigger than a giant's nose. Here they found a place where they were pushed forward at the speed of the tanker with no effort at all. For a short time they weaved to and fro crossing each other's paths like skiers on a fast downhill run. Every so often they had to go to the

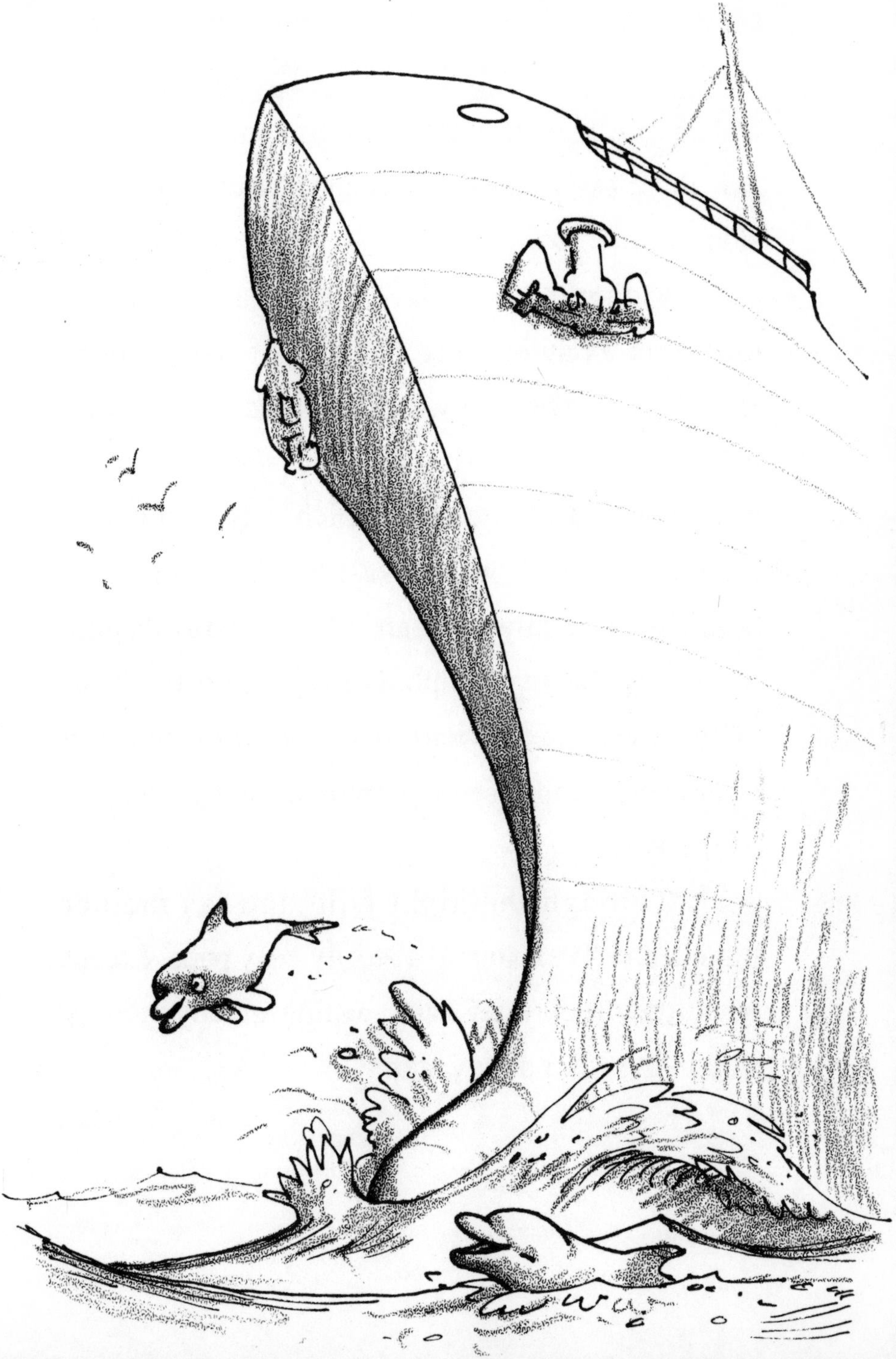

surface to breathe and when they did so they jumped clear out of the sea. The bows of the tanker rose like steel cliffs. High above them they saw the massive anchor suspended from the ship's side.

Riding the bow wave of the tanker was not the same as swimming in front of the friendly Blue whale. The ship was rigid; it had no warmth, no soul and no sensitivity. Dilo and his mother were dwarfed by the hulk which was as big as a floating island. It was so vast that the humans on board were totally unaware of the joyful display put on by the two dolphins playing on the bow. When their games were over mother and son swam away unnoticed to continue their journey to Seal Island.

Through the night Dilo and his mother travelled on, keeping up a steady easy pace, except when they took brief naps, resting quietly side by side in the calm dark water.

9 Feeding frenzy

The sun rose. Dilo sent out his magic sound-echo and a new signal came back. The sea was getting shallower. They were approaching land. When the dolphin surfaced, he could see mountains far away on the horizon. Also in the distance he saw a great mass of birds wheeling around and around in the sky. Dilo's mother had already spotted them.

She told her son to swim on the surface and watch them. The young dolphin knew something unusual was happening because the sea was full of sounds and vibrations he had not heard before. They affected him and he felt a strange tingle of excitement. Dilo and his mother stayed side by side but increased their pace.

Swimming on the surface, Dilo watched the birds with his eyes. He saw some of them drop out of the sky. At the very last moment before they hit the water they closed their wings. With their pointed beaks stretched out in front of them, and their bodies arrow-straight, the birds split the surface and vanished into the sea below.

"They are feeding," said Dilo's mother.

"I'm hungry," replied Dilo, feeling the excitement that was building up inside him getting stronger and stronger.

Faster and faster went the two dolphins. They swam close to the surface jumping across the waves like racehorses, to gain extra speed. The noise in the sea grew louder and louder as Dilo and his mother rushed forwards as fast at they could go.

Dilo quickly understood the reason for the presence and behaviour of the birds for he found himself in the midst of a gigantic shoal of tiny fish. They were so close together it seemed as though the sea was almost solid with them. They moved as if they were all linked together. They swept up from the depths and the surface of the sea boiled briefly as hundreds of them jumped into the air.

Then Dilo realised why they were in such a frenzy. Big fish shot up from below. They tore into the silver cloud snapping at the tiny fish and gobbling them down in a flash. Some of the small fish were chopped in two. Before the broken pieces had time to sink very far they were snapped up by other big fish that rocketed up from the

depths and then plunged back down again.

All around him gannets dropped out of the sky like hailstones, grabbing fish in their beaks and gobbling them down head first. As soon as one had swallowed a fish it took to the air and flew high into the sky only to plummet back into the sea again just a few seconds later.

The two dolphins hurled themselves into the silver cloud and snapped up the small fish one after another. Both Dilo and his mother were very hungry after their long swim and they ate voraciously. They followed the great swarm of fish as it billowed and wheeled, constantly changing shape but always staying as a single mass. If any single fish got separated from the cloud it panicked and would flash like a piece of silver paper in the sunlight. Usually it was snapped-up as it desperately tried to rejoin the shoal.

So engrossed in their hunt were Dilo and his mother that they did not notice a change taking place. The big fish stopped darting up from below. The small fish formed into a tight ball. Dilo and his mother circled them. Suddenly they heard a deep sound coming from far below. Dilo's mood changed in an instant. He rushed to his mother's side and stayed very close to her. The sound filled him with excitement and apprehension. He felt as though it was signalling the beginning of a momentous and frightening event. Which indeed it was.

10 Kings of the ocean

The water was so full of sound that Dilo's body seemed to vibrate. He beamed his own sound down into the depths but the other sound was so great that he could hardly make out the images. He could just distinguish fast-moving fish. But beneath them were large shapes that were coming up towards him.

The sound grew louder and louder. When he touched his mother's side he could feel her body quivering. It was as if the whole ocean was alive with sound.

Then the large fish he had seen earlier suddenly reappeared in panic-stricken confusion. They darted from the deep blue depths and shot in all directions ignoring the large ball of small fish wheeling in bewilderment.

The predators had become the prey.

From underneath, rushing towards them, came the huge, black bodies of the killer whales or orcas. Dilo was aware of the brilliant white patches behind their eyes. They swept up from the depths with such speed and awesome power that the previously impressive looking fish now seemed insignificant. The lower jaws of the orcas were a startling white. The rims of their opened mouths were lined with a single row of large, conical, ivory teeth, which snapped shut onto their luckless victims. The fish were flipped so that their heads were pointing into the throats of their captors. Then, with a gulp, they disappeared.

The shoal of small fish, which had re-formed into a tight ball before the orcas arrived, burst. Splinters of glinting silver flew in all directions as if blown apart by an explosion. There was mayhem under the sea.

The sight of thousands of confused fish rushing in all directions triggered in Dilo and his mother a reaction they could not control. For a short time the two dolphins were overwhelmed by

their hunting instincts which came upon them like a bout of madness. They pushed forward snapping up the bewildered fish that zig-zagged about them. They were so engrossed by the hunt, the sounds all around them and the confusion, that they took no notice of a new presence. More predators had come from the deep water to join the carnage. The new arrivals were bigger than the fish that had first appeared but were smaller than the orcas. They moved swiftly and silently with deceptively lazy movements of their powerful tails. They sliced through the water with effortless ease. These were not wriggling fish. Their high dorsal fins stabilised their passage. They moved as smoothly as gliding gulls. Their long pectoral fins, angled from their strong bodies and acting as hydrofoils, enabled them to bank steeply. Their heads were sharply pointed and their upper jaws extended well beyond their lower jaws. Their eyes were cold and alert. So efficiently did the sharks pass through the water that they hardly deviated from their course to take a fleeing fish. Dilo noticed the head of an extra large shark twist sharply sideways as it snapped at a fish that might otherwise have escaped the malevolent jaws lined with rows of small razor-sharp teeth. More sharks appeared in quick succession. They roamed with consummate ease and impressive power through the distended shoal of small fish.

Like an undersea snowstorm the entire sea was filled with countless tiny, darting fish. Sometimes a group would come together in a line and flow like a stream only to be broken apart by the sharks soaring through them. With barely perceptible changes of movement in their power glides the sharks intercepted their victims and plucked them from the teeming frightened shoals.

One shark swooped and with a snap of its jaws chopped a large fish in half. The head vanished and the tail portion started to drift down -

a single slowly moving object in a world where everything was in a frenzy. Another shark banked steeply and bore down on the tempting morsel. The broken fish was removed from the scene.

A much larger fish, wounded by one of the orcas but not captured, was dispatched by the sharks. They bit chunks from it before one of them grabbed the remainder in its jaws, accelerated to full speed, and hurtled out of sight into the depths,

Although the sharks were impressive they were dwarfed in size, speed, power and beauty by the orcas who moved through the incredible scene in pursuit of their own food. Sometimes the orcas took small fish, sometimes larger ones. At all times they appeared to have a complete disregard for the sharks. The orcas were the kings of the ocean, and they knew it. They tolerated the sharks. They allowed them to be present to clean up after them. They also permitted Dilo and his mother to join in their feast.

Such was the confusion and noise in the sea that Dilo thought every orca was feeding with complete disregard for the others. But as the hunt progressed Dilo became aware that this wasn't so. There were a dozen orcas involved and those on the outside were herding the fish towards the middle, keeping them concentrated in a small volume of sea. If fish showed signs of escaping one of the inner orcas would sweep round and drive it towards one of the circling orcas, who would then rush forward and snap-up the fish before it gained it's freedom.

Dilo and his mother drifted near the surface at the centre of the melée. Dilo looked down. A huge shoal of small fish had gathered beneath him. It had the appearance of a giant silver cloud suspended in the sea, blown by an unseen wind that caused it to move. Although it often billowed, the edges always remained sharply defined. As he watched and wondered, Dilo saw a hole appear in the middle of the cloud and through it shot a large fish. A fraction of a second later the hole had expanded to become a huge circle. Through its centre, in hot pursuit of a large fish, came the black and white head of an orca.

Dilo watched, transfixed by the sight of the open mouth of the mighty orca whose white lower jaw contrasted with its jet black head. There was a very brief flash of white teeth before the mouth snapped shut. The small, petrified dolphin was aware of a blur of black and white speeding past towards the sky.

An instant later the orca burst through the surface of the sea with the fish firmly locked in its mouth. Foaming water cascaded down the body of the giant as it reared out of the sea. Then it crashed back into the water in a seething mass of foam. The huge black dorsal fin cut through the water like a sword before it vanished beneath the surface. Then a gigantic tail fluke appeared. The black topside glistened like porcelain as it rose out of the water. The white underside shone briefly before it thrashed down on to the surface of the sea with a slap that sent a shock wave tearing into the depths.

The force that had held the shoal of fishes together was once again shattered. Some of them rushed up in confusion and skittered across the sea, rippling its placid surface. Many were snatched from the water by the ever-increasing number of birds that had gathered and were swooping down from the sky.

When the orcas had taken their fill the sound which had filled the water died quite suddenly. The birds stopped dropping from the sky. The sharks vanished as quickly as they had come. The dispersed fry started to collect in small shoals that drifted nervously into deeper water.

The orcas grouped into close formation and the regal procession moved away. At short intervals they broke the surface and the high dorsal fins of the males could be seen straight, upright and proud, alongside the smaller recurved fins of the females. Because of their size and the

ease with which they moved through the water
they appeared to be travelling slowly, but that was
an illusion. Before long they were far away.

11   Seal Island

By the time the Orcas were out of sight the madness of the feeding frenzy had completely left the two dolphins. Dilo swam quietly to his mother's side. What had overcome them? It was as if another force from outside had taken complete control. Now it had gone Dilo became aware of himself and his mother. The sea seemed unnaturally quiet. He listened intently, but there were no distinct sounds - only a background hum. All other forms of life had vanished. The sea and sky were empty. Dilo and his mother were alone again in a vast ocean.

In the far distance the sea was joined to the sky by a jagged grey strip. Like two travellers moving through the emptiness of space the dolphins headed towards the alien land on the horizon.

As the sun set the wind dropped completely. The surface of the sea was flat calm. Every time the two dolphins surfaced the sharp sound of their breaths spread out across the water and vanished into the silence. When dusk turned to darkness, Dilo and his mother continued their journey towards Seal Island at a steady pace.

At dawn Dilo sent out a sound beam and the signal came back giving him a sound picture of the rocks below. When he surfaced, he could see the light shining on the cliffs of Seal Island. A gentle wind ruffled the sea. The sun glinted on the small waves. Dilo felt good inside. He was still full of food. Everything was peaceful. Dilo's mother decided they would have a lazy day quietly exploring the rocks that rose from the sea bed and the currents that flowed around them. A young seal came to greet them. Excitedly it circled the new arrivals and then headed towards the island, hotly pursued by Dilo. The seal was extremely agile. From the way it pirouetted and hung in the water it was obvious that it wanted to play.

Soon the two young mammals were flying
backwards and forwards past Dilo's mother, who
was finding it hard to resist joining in. The seal
whizzed past her like an arrow closely followed by
Dilo whose tail was pumping up and down at full
speed. When Dilo caught-up with the seal he
nipped it playfully. The seal turned round
instantly. A moment later the two playmates were
racing back past Dilo's mother in the opposite
direction. But this time the seal was chasing Dilo.

85

Running short of breath Dilo headed upwards. The seal caught-up just as the dolphin reached the surface. The two jumped together. Bumping in mid flight they fell back into the water with a glorious splash.

Dilo's mother watched their antics from below. Now they were heading straight for her, again at full speed. The seal let out a stream of bubbles from its nostrils. Dilo, who was close behind, rocketed through them.

"I can do that too," thought Dilo.

He rushed past the seal deep down to the seabed and stopped. Just as the seal caught up Dilo let out a burst of air through his blowhole. For a brief moment the seal was engulfed, splitting the balloon of air into a cascade of tiny, sparkling bubbles. Delighted with the effect the dolphin accelerated towards the surface, chased by the seal. This time they leapt out of the water separately and sped back into the depths in different directions.

Dilo decided it was time for a new game - one he had often played with his mother. He zoomed back and forth, well below the depths at which the big seaweeds grew, until he found a deep gulley with an overhanging rock. Hovering close to the wall, and hidden from above, he stopped and waited.

In the quiet stillness he became aware of everything around him. The rocks were completely covered in what looked like tiny flowers. The more closely he studied them the more beautiful and intricate they appeared. The colours of the sea anemones that grew in profusion were exquisite. Dilo felt as if he was in a jewel box. Lost in wonderment he forgot all about the game.

"What was it my mother told me?" he asked himself.

"Always be prepared to catch a moment of beauty."

He had made a discovery and would have to show her this special place where flowers grew on the walls. As he drifted slowly forward he spotted a cluster of plants that were different and even more delicate that the sea anemones. The feather-like tentacles of the tubeworms, as they are known to humans, grew out of tubes to form petals with circular bands of colour.The delicate flowers waved back and forth as if blown by a gentle wind. Still in a dream Dilo moved slowly forward to stroke the flowers with the tip of his beak.

Just as he was about to make contact they all vanished in an instant with a quiet "plop". It happened so quickly he didn't see them go. Now all that was left was a collection of thin grey plant pots that were not very attractive.

The sudden disappearance of the tubeworms brought Dilo out of his reveries.

"H'mm, these Plop-Plop plants are very sensitive," he said to himself.

At that moment his seal friend swam excitedly into view and their game of hide and seek began in ernest. Dilo turned round so he couldn't see where the seal went to hide, although he did sneak a quick look to see in which direction it headed.

A few moments later the young dolphin left his gulley to search for his friend. He swam up to the seaweed forest that covered most of the rocks in shallow water but there was no sign of the seal. Dilo stopped and listened. He scanned the area with the special sound his mother had taught him to use for what she termed "investigational purposes". He got a very weak signal from in the kelp. So he kept sending out the sound and headed towards the place where it seemed to be coming from.

The seal hiding under the seaweed could hear Dilo's signal. It stayed absolutely still. Then it blew out a tiny stream of air through its nose. The bubbles jostled through the seaweed canopy before breaking through into the clear waters above. Dilo picked up the clue immediately. A few moments later he was nosing down into the dense seaweed called kelp which has long, leathery stalks.

Plucking up courage he plunged down into it and found himself in a strange world. He was in a forest. The kelp stalks were like thin tree trunks holding up a thick roof of olive green leaves that blocked out everything above from view. The kelp trees were anchored to the rocks by what looked like masses of twisted roots. The floor of the forest, which was very uneven, was completely covered with encrustations in various hues of soft pink. It was certainly mysterious; but surprisingly it wasn't dark and it wasn't frightening. There seemed to be an inner glow of pale light that somehow made Dilo feel unafraid.

Browsing creatures called sea urchins in many different shades ranging from red-brown to violet-blue, were scattered everywhere. They were about the size of tennis balls and were covered with small white spines. Some were decorated with broken fragments of shells and small pieces of seaweed.

Although the seal knew the dolphin was on his way it was still surprised when Dilo suddenly came into view. The startled seal dislodged a sea urchin feeding on a heavy kelp trunk. Dilo watched the prickly ball drift gently down and bounce in slow motion. It came to rest close to a starfish - to which it was related - rather like the dolphins are to the big whales. Dilo didn't know this of course, but he did feel instinctively that everything around him was linked together in a very magical way. Indeed everything around him seemed magical.

Dilo decided Seal Island really was a special place. What made it even better was that he had found a young friend who loved to play games. But it was time to go back to his mother who he thought would be getting anxious.

He pushed up through the rubbery blades of kelp that slid easily over his body into the bright early morning sunlight. The water was extremely clear. Dilo didn't have to use his echo-sound to find his mother. In the distance he saw her cruising slowly round a pinnacle of rock that rose almost to the surface. She didn't look at all anxious.

The seal swam off to find its own mother as Dilo rejoined his. He told her excitedly about the wonderful things he had seen - especially the Plop-Plop plants. He insisted she should see them for herself and led her down to the deep gulley. The Plop-Plop flowers had come back out. This time Dilo didn't attempt to stroke them. His mother explained that they weren't flowers at all - but were really animals. And that was one of the reasons why they could move so quickly.

She was pleased her son was so sensitive and curious. To show her love she swam past him gently stroking him with her pectoral fin. Dilo wiggled with pleasure.

"It's time to move on, don't you think?" she said, leading the way back into open water.

The two dolphins swam towards a headland that ran far out into the sea. Dilo's mother knew that they would find plenty of food there especially when the tide was running fast. But as they came to the tip of the headland Dilo's mother heard a sound that made her call her son to her

side. The sound was not unpleasant. Indeed it was
an interesting one. All the same deep down she
had an uneasy feeling. She swam alongside and
gently stroked him with her flipper. Dilo enjoyed
feeling his mother's caress and stayed close to her.

12 The net

Dilo's mother searched her memory. Where had she heard that sound before? Suddenly she remembered the link. It was similar to the one she had heard round about the time her companion had been killed - before Dilo was born. She and Dilo listened to the sound carefully. It was not a natural sound - it was too regular for that. It was like a heartbeat only thousands of times more powerful. She felt a strong desire to swim towards it. The sound was calling her, but the uneasy feeling persisted. Suddenly she knew why. When she was very young she had been warned about a sound that lured dolphins and sometimes brought disaster to those who answered the call.

She told Dilo about the mysterious sound. Even so she felt excited. She gave Dilo a playful flip with her tail and swam away. Dilo knew that was the sign for a game. He chased after her. Dilo's mother leapt high into the air and crashed down into the sea with the biggest splash she could make. Dilo followed her but couldn't jump so high. The joy of the game filled both of them. They rushed along the surface and dived. Through the green water they rushed, sometimes side by side, sometimes in line. They were so engrossed in their game they forgot about the sound. The two dolphins didn't think about anything around them. They were so full of joy and energy that the rest of the world did not exist.

Dilo's mother swam fast over the top of her son and finned at full speed towards the point where the land ran into the ocean. Dilo was following behind her when suddenly she stopped. Her body swung sideways and Dilo bumped into her. Their game came to an abrupt end. Dilo's mother thrashed with her tail and twisted her body with all her strength but she did not move away. Dilo hung motionless in the water not knowing what to do. What had happened to his mother? It was the first time she had behaved liked this.

Dilo switched on his magic sound and it showed his mother was caught in the middle of an almost invisible barrier. Like a fly in a spider's web, his mother was caught in a monofilament fishing net that stretched out from the headland far into the sea.

Dilo's mother stayed still. She did not know what to do either. Dilo swam up to her and touched her with his fin. She was comforted by him. She decided to take stock of the situation and sent out her own magic sound to see what was holding her. When she looked carefully with her sound, she could see the net faintly but clearly. Some distance away she could see a fish. It too was caught in the net and struggled to free itself. But without success. The fish's gills were open wide and Dilo's mother knew it was dying. She also knew that she too would die soon if she did not get to the surface for air.

As well as her troubles, another problem was forcing itself on her. Again she could hear the mysterious sound she had forgotten about. It was getting louder. And that meant it was getting closer. Her son was in danger from whatever was making the sound.

"Dilo, you must go away," she said to her son.

"No, I cannot leave you," he replied. "I must stay and help you."

"No. You must go," she insisted. "There is too much danger here. Go away. Please go away," she begged.

But Dilo would not leave.

The sea around Dilo's mother was calm. It was also full of beautiful sounds. Two dolphins slowly appeared. They were the ghosts of the companions she had last seen alive, just before Dilo was born. One of them drifted slowly past.

"We have come to take you on another step of your journey - into the next world," the dolphin said. "When we get there we shall all be together again."

Dilo's mother felt a gentle joy flow through her body. She had missed her friends so much.

Then her feelings of pleasure stopped.

"But what about Dilo?" she asked. "He is coming with me, isn't he?"

"No, not yet," came the reply. "He must stay here."

Dilo's mother looked around for her son. As he swam slowly towards her she saw that Dilo was bathed with golden light.

"He is a very special dolphin," her companion continued. "That is why Dilo has a star on his dorsal fin. He has a mission."

Dilo's mother felt her son stroking her gently. Again she tried to tell him to go away.

She decided to have one last attempt at freeing herself from the net. Using what was left of her energy she thrashed her tail with all her might. She felt the net giving as she moved up towards the surface. For a moment she thought she was free. Then another piece of the net wrapped itself round her tail. Although she had made a hole in the net she was held more tightly than ever. She became quite still.

Although she could feel him touching her, it seemed as if Dilo was getting further and further away. He was slowly going to the end of a tunnel, getting smaller and smaller. He became a point. The tunnel closed. She was dead.

Dilo stayed beside his mother and tried to push her to the surface. As he did so the mysterious noise got closer and closer. Then it changed. Lots of new sounds came down from above, sounds he had never heard before. The net that held his mother prisoner started to move. He swam to the surface and saw the fishing boat. The net was being winched onboard. He could hear the men talking. One of them shouted and pointed at Dilo who quickly submerged. His mother was moving. She was being hauled up with the net. Dilo stayed beside her. When she reached the surface the net stopped moving. Dilo swam beside the boat.

The men were very angry when they saw the damage the dolphin had done to their net, and they tried to untangle it from Dilo's mother but could not get her out completely. So they cursed and cut the net.

Still partly wrapped in the almost invisible nylon net that had trapped and killed her, Dilo's mother slowly sank towards the seabed.

The tide was starting to run and the body was moving away from the land. Dilo stayed beside his mother until at last he had to go to the surface to breathe.

As the tidal race built up it took Dilo's mother with it into deep water where the current became slower. Eventually she came to rest in a rocky gully with sea coral fans growing like delicate pink bushes along the walls. It was a beautiful, quiet place.

Dilo stayed looking at his mother resting silently, peacefully. That was how he would remember her. He would also remember the joyful times they had together.

The sun was setting when Dilo finally left his mother. The sea was calm. He cruised very slowly just below the surface. He stayed down as long as he could between breaths. He had a lot to think about. He did not feel lonely. She had told him he was a nomad. Somehow just gliding through the water eased the pain he felt inside. Although she was not beside him he could feel her spirit. It was in the water all around him.

He knew he would have to follow the Call of the Deep. But, now he would have to do it on his own.

Dilo was well away from the land when night fell. He cruised slowly to a stop and rested on the surface. The air was still. The sea hardly moved. It was very quiet. All around the water was flat. He felt as if he was in the middle of a huge circle of sea. Overhead was the dome of the sky - velvet black and dusted with stars. He looked at it full of wonder. He noticed that some of the stars were grouped in patterns. And then he saw her. Outlined in stars his mother was silently watching over him.

As he gazed at her he sent a message telling her how much he loved her and that he was safe. At that moment he knew if ever he felt lost or lonely she would be there in the heavens to guide him. He closed his eyes and took a brief peaceful sleep. He had a long journey ahead of him.

The End

Author *Horace Dobbs*
with friendly wild
dolphin off
Amble,
Northumberland

Horace Dobbs is uniquely qualified to write this book because he himself has been beckoned by the 'call of the deep'. He has dived in all the oceans of the world and has made a special study of dolphins. Virtually all of the encounters Dilo has while growing up Horace has also experienced: he has been in the middle of a shark feeding frenzy, dived with seals and fanned scallops with his fins until they rose from the seabed and were swimming around him by rapidly opening and closing their shells. At the time he was wearing full diving equipment and was so amused by the incident that he sat on the seabed and conducted the underwater ballet of the Clop-Clops with his snorkel tube.

Horace has a wonderful gift for recounting such adventures, and has enthralled live audiences of all ages - including children with learning difficulties.

Horace Dobbs is the author of numerous books. In addition to presenting his own films Horace is a popular interviewee on radio and TV.

106

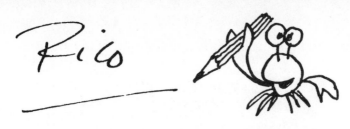

Rico is the pen name of the artist and photographer *Richard Oldfield* whose highly acclaimed work is published world-wide. His greatest love is the undersea world, of which, as a widely experienced diver, he has an intimate knowledge. His studies of how light interacts with water are reflected in his stunning paintings of marine subjects.

Rico has worked with Horace Dobbs on a number of assignments. He sketched this cartoon when they were filming a TV feature about a friendly wild dolphin who was generating a booming trade for the local boatmen.

Rico has had a regular cartoon strip in *DIVER* for over 20 years and it is to his feature that most readers turn to when they first open the magazine.

Price £2.95

Size: 298 x 210mm

Full colour card cover.

14 pages. Illustrated

throughout by Rico.

Publisher: Watch

Publishing (1994)

ISBN: 0-9522389-1-8

Dilo's Fun and Activities Book

High quality activity book that will keep children of all ages occupied. Design a T-shirt, do the dolphin wordsearch, battle through the anatomy anagrams or simply join the dots and colouring the pictures.

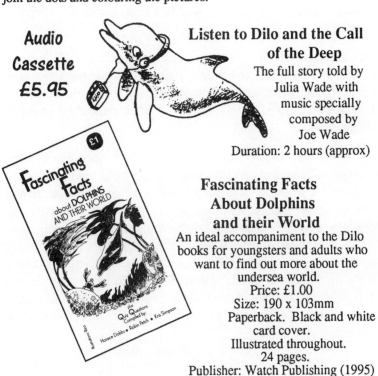

Audio Cassette £5.95

Listen to Dilo and the Call of the Deep

The full story told by Julia Wade with music specially composed by Joe Wade

Duration: 2 hours (approx)

Fascinating Facts About Dolphins and their World

An ideal accompaniment to the Dilo books for youngsters and adults who want to find out more about the undersea world.

Price: £1.00

Size: 190 x 103mm

Paperback. Black and white card cover.

Illustrated throughout.

24 pages.

Publisher: Watch Publishing (1995)

ISBN: 0-95-22389-4-2

All available from: International Dolphin Watch

10 Melton Road, North Ferriby, E. Yorks HU14 3ET England

Tel: 01482632990   Fax: 01482 634914

Please add 50p P&P per item

Letter from the author

Dear Reader

Since the first edition of this book was published in 1994 Dilo has grown. In 1996 *Dilo and the Call of the Deep* was published in Japan. The Japanese edition is quite different to the English version. As is the practice in Japan, the front cover corresponds to the back cover of the western version. The script is in vertical lines that scan from right to left. The illustrations were also drawn in a completely different style by Takayuki Terakado.

When a dear friend of mine, Shizuko Ouwehand, read the book in Japanese to her husband, she cried with emotion at the beautiful and poetic way the text had been translated by Sakae Hemmi.

One outcome of the Japanese version is that the overall concept of Dilo is now richer and fuller. This set me thinking about how much more wisdom and knowledge of dolphins might be brought to light if the Dilo stories were published in other languages.

My dream now is to get my Dilo stories transcribed into as wide a range of languages and art forms as possible. For instance, I would love to see a Dilo story translated into his or her native tongue by an Innuit (Eskimo) poet. Imagine the illustrations done by a native American Indian who also carves totem poles, or an Australian Aborigine who paints didgeridoos. My dream is already beginning to unfold. I am in contact with a famous Zulu story teller in South Africa. But I need more help. If you can think of any ways we can spread Dilo's message please contact me via Watch Publishing. I shall look forward to receiving your ideas.

Yours sincerely

Please pass this book to a friend to read

If you don't want to part with this book

you could have one sent

directly from

International Dolphin Watch

P.G.
This book should only be read by children
under the age of eighty.